P9-ASB-522

DATE DUE

Demco No. 62-0549

Live the Dream . . .

This is the compelling story of Maggie Callahan's captivity among the Seneca Indians during the American Revolution.

Here is a chance to step back 200 years, into an era filled with danger and mystery and incredible beauty.

Maggie's tale is a rich blend of heart-pounding adventure, interpretive history and good, old-fashioned storytelling, created especially for children and dreamers of all ages.

Maggie Among The Seneca

INDIAN CAPTIVITY
ON THE AMERICAN FRONTIER

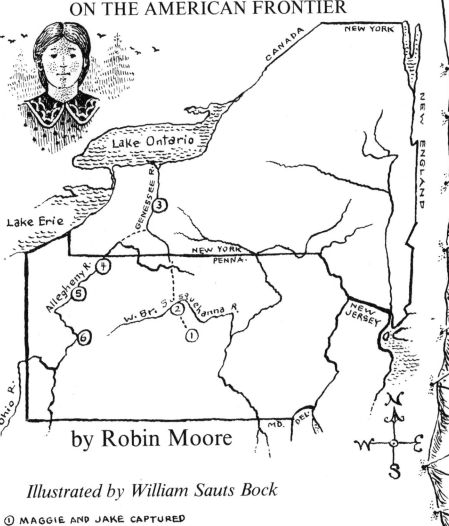

by Robin Moore

Illustrated by William Sauts Bock

① MAGGIE AND JAKE CAPTURED
② JAKE ESCAPES HERE
③ LITTLE BEARD'S VILLAGE
④ ELK HUNTING CAMP
⑤ VILLAGE OF BUCCALOONS
⑥ FRANNY'S TAVERN IN KITTANNING

Table of Contents

LIBRARY OF CONGRESS CATALOG NO. 87-81622

ISBN 0-9613433-3-8

This book is dedicated to:

My father, Robert C. Moore

and

My son, Jesse S. Moore

In their own way, each has taught me to love the things that are wild and free . . .

Introduction

This is the story of Maggie Callahan's captivity among the Seneca Indians of Up-State New York during the Revolutionary War.

While this tale is fictional, it is based upon the true experiences of hundreds of frontier women who were taken captive and lived among the Iroquois during the Revolution.

I want you to enjoy the story. In order to do that, you are going to need to know some things about the Seneca people and about the historical events which shaped their lives.

Because I am primarily a storyteller and not a historian, and because I was not skillful enough to include the historical information without disrupting the flow of the story, I made a storyteller's choice: I will outline the background information in this introduction and let the story stand on its own. If you would like to learn more about the Seneca and about their role in the American Revolution, a list of excellent books appears at the end of this section.

Of all the tribes on the colonial frontier, the Seneca were perhaps the most fascinating. Historian Anthony Wallace writes, "To be a Seneca was to be a member of the most feared, most courted and most respected Indian tribe in North America."

The Seneca were the largest and most powerful of the five tribes which made up the Iroquois Confederacy. The Confederacy, or The Great League, as it was sometimes called, bound together all the Indian people living in the region we now know as New York State. But their influence spread much wider. Trade, diplomatic and war missions carried them from Canada to the Carolinas, from the Atlantic Ocean to the Mississippi River.

Lewis Henry Morgan, author of the classic study on the Seneca, noted: "They achieved for themselves a more remarkable civil organization, and acquired a higher degree of influence, than any other race of Indian lineage, except those of Mexico and Peru. In the drama of European colonization, they stood for nearly two centuries with an unshaken front."

It is little wonder that the Europeans who came to this country stood in awe of the power and influence exerted by the Iroquois. We now know that the political structure of the Confederacy was used as a model by the founding fathers in creating the American democracy.

It was inevitable that the Iroquois would become involved in the wars Europeans waged on this soil. While the Confederacy attempted to maintain a neutral position, cleverly playing each side off against the other, they were eventually drawn into two disasterous wars: The French and Indian War and the American Revolution. Unfortunately, in both cases, they picked the losing side.

Maggie comes among the Seneca during the last chapter of this drama. During the Revolution, the Seneca, and most of the other Iroquois, had aligned themselves with the British, who fought against the rebellious American colonists.

The Seneca warriors became useful tools for the British forces. Indian raiding parties drove American settlers out of their wilderness homes and created a general panic on the frontier during their raids in the summer of 1778. In Central Pennsylvania, this period was referred to as "The Great Runaway." It is during one of these raids that Maggie is captured and carried north to the Seneca

Country.

Maggie had no way of knowing the role war captives played in Seneca life. To the Seneca, prisoners were an important byproduct of warfare. When the captives were brought to the home village, weak or unacceptable prisoners would be killed outright or tortured to death.

While much has been made of the terrible tortures Indians were capable of imposing on their victims, little has been said about the adoption system which acted in the prisoner's behalf.

It is a matter of historical record that many frontier women were not killed by their captors but adopted and became productive members of Seneca society. In many cases, when the captured women had an opportunity to return to their homes, they elected to stay with their Indian families. Mary Jemison and Francis Slocum are two Pennsylvania women who serve as examples.

Why did these women prefer Seneca society to their former life in the colonies? Part of the answer lies in the roles women occupied in these radically different cultures.

Few in the history of human civilization enjoyed as much control over their own lives as the Seneca woman. Women in Seneca society had the power to start and end wars, depose leaders and divorce their husbands at will. A matriarchal society, the Seneca lineage was passed down through the female side of the family. Families were organized into clans. Marriages, arranged by the mothers, had to be outside the clan.

Women had strong economic power because they were responsible for the agriculture which fed their people. Seneca women enjoyed a role of power and influence in the domestic sphere, free from interference by the men.

At the same time, men had their own, complementary, sphere of influence: in the woods and on the trails criss-crossing the Iroquois land. Men were often gone on hunting, trapping, war or diplomatic missions.

Women and men moved in a time and place where gender-defined roles made sense and allowed families to live together in relative harmony.

Little Beard's Village, along the Genesee River in Up-State New York, was a sterling example of the kind of world the Seneca women were able to build. Before General John Sullivan led his colonial army down to burn the village, he said to his men, "This is probably the most beautiful place in America."

Morgan refers to Sullivan's sweep through the Iroquois Country as "The Holocaust." To the Confederacy, it certainly was. The Seneca never recovered from the destruction caused by Sullivan's Raid in the summer of 1779. This was truly the beginning of the end. In a short time, they became refugees in the land they once called their own.

Although Little Beard's village is gone, the Genesee Valley is still there, as beautiful as ever. During my research trip for this book, I was able to find the old village site along the banks of the Genesee. Today it is still as it was: acres and acres of lush corn and bean fields growing in the rich black loam deposited by the river.

One hot, cloudy, summer evening, I walked for hours in the corn along the river. Coming down along the river, I found raccoon tracks in the mud. I smiled as I wondered how many generations of raccoons had been stealing corn on warm summer nights along the Genesee. Some things do not change.

Incidentally, the Seneca name for Little Beard's town was De-o-nun-da-ga-a. But I have chosen to use the English name as a way of making the story more accessible to most readers. Similarly, I have used the English names for people and places throughout. Maggie never learns to speak the language.

I would like to thank the people who helped me make this book.

William Sauts Bock's wonderful illustrations have added immeasurably to the book. I know of no one who can make the characters come alive as he can. Thanks to

Bill for his help and encouragement.

I have received important editorial help from my compatriots Betty Schoen and Judy Foulke. I thank them for their careful reading and insightful comments on the story as it moved through successive drafts.

A special thanks to The New York Historical Society of Cooperstown, New York for providing me with copies of obscure documents relating to Sullivan's Raid. I also thank the Rosenbach Institute of Philadelphia for allowing me to peruse their rare book collection, which included narratives of Indian captivity.

I thank my wife Jacqueline for patiently reading my drafts each night and sending me back to the typewriter each morning with the renewed confidence that this is a magical story, worth telling. I thank my children, Jesse and Rachel, for their perfect interruptions.

Most of all, I'm deeply appreciative to the many readers who flattered, threatened and prodded me into writing a sequel to *The Bread Sister*. Their enthusiasm carried me through the lonely job of writing down this story.

Thanks to Maggie, that strong-hearted woman inside of me. She constantly amazes me with her courage, tenacity and resilience in the face of overwhelming odds.

Like the first book in this series, *Maggie Among The Seneca* is designed to be read aloud, in the old-fashioned tradition of family evenings by the hearthfire. Each chapter is about a night's worth of reading. You might want to do it that way.

Enjoy the story. Live the dream.

Robin Moore

For Further Reading:

League of The Iroquois, Henry Lewis Morgan, Citadel Press, Secaucus, New Jersey, 1962

The Death and Rebirth of the Seneca, Anthony F.C. Wallace, Vintage Books, New York, 1969

The Life of Mary Jemison, James A. Seaver, The American Scenic and Historic Preservation Society, New York, 1963

Land of the Senecas, Arch Merrill, Empire State Books, 1949

The Iroquois Trail, M.R. Harrington, Rutgers University Press, New Brunswick, New Jersey, 1965

Major General Sullivan's Official Report, New York State Historical Association, Cooperstown, New York

The Wilderness War, Allan W. Eckert, Bantam Books, New York, 1978

Chapter 1

It was a warm summer night, crickets singing, owls hooting in the pine branches overhead, no moon.

Maggie Callahan and Old Jake Logan sat up by their fire, bone-weary from walking all day. They had been traveling hard for four days now, crossing the seven mountain ridges, headed west, out of Pennsylvania and toward the Ohio River Country.

Maggie sat with her back up against a tree, staring into the fire. She was a fine-looking girl, sixteen years old that summer, Irish, her hair red like fire, the lines of her face cut sure and clear. She was wearing simple clothes: an ankle-length dress and shortblouse, an apron with her sheath knife tucked into the waistband, elkhide moccasins.

She stared across the fire at the old man, watching him as he laid some kindling wood on the flames. It was him, more than anyone, who had kept her alive since she had first come to the frontier, two years before.

She grinned, remembering how scared she had been of him that first day, when he had slipped up on her at her aunt's abandoned cabin.

He was the wildest-looking character she had ever seen: dressed head to toe in smoke-stained buckskins, rifle carried in the crook of his arm, hair and long beard wild like the wind.

"Jake," she said at last, "what are the chances of us finding her?"

The old man looked up from the flames. "Yer Aunt Franny? Oh, we'll find 'er, don't you worry 'bout that. I'll bet my eyebrows on it."

"But I thought you told me that when folks went west, they were gone for good, never to be found again."

"Well, that's gen'rally true. But I think it'll be different with Franny and yer Uncle Thomas."

"Why do you say that?"

"Think about it fer a minute. When they lived back in Penns Valley, didn't everybody know 'em fer miles around?"

Maggie had to admit he was right.

"And why was zat?"

Maggie didn't have to think hard on that one.

"It was because of Franny's bread-bakin'," she said. "You said yourself, people would come from all over for a taste of that Callahan bread."

The old man nodded. "Now that's 'zackly what I mean. Don't it start to make sense now? I figure if Franny's still bakin' that bread, folks out in the Ohio will know about it. We'll jist start askin' around and let the reputation of that bread lead us right to 'em."

Maggie nodded. She had to admit, Jake had a point.

Just then they were startled by a shout that came from the main trail, down along the creekbed.

"Ho!" the voice said, "Kin ya share yer fire with an ol' fella?"

Jake reached out and snatched up his long-barreled flintlock rifle. He and Maggie scuttled back out of the ring of firelight.

"Ho!" the voice shouted again, "Got two squirrels here, be glad to share with ya."

"Step ahead," Jake shouted, "up inta the firelight, let's git a look at ya."

"Comin' in," the man said amiably, "comin' in. Don't blame you folks fer bein' careful. If a stranger walked up on my camp at night, I'd do the same."

He was coming up into the firelight now. Maggie could see that he was old, even older than Jake. Maybe sixty winters. Carried on his boney shoulders were a hunter's shooting pouch and a blanket roll. He carried a flintlock, like Jake's, and was dressed in buckskins. He wore a slouchy felt hat and from the looks of his lower jaw, he didn't have a tooth in his mouth. He limped a little.

Jake squinted into the firelight. "Gimp, is zat you?"

The old man squinted back. "Well, a'course it's me. Who in creation are you?"

Jake came up into the firelight. "Ya couldn't fergit this face, couldya?"

The old fellow laughed. "Logan, you old dog!"

The two men shook hands warmly. Jake put his arm around the older and turned to Maggie.

"It's all right, girl. This here's Gimpy Weaver, an' old huntin' partner o' mine and a sure-enough mountain man."

Maggie came up into the light. Gimpy took off his hat.

"Glad to meet ya, miss." He turned to Jake. "Is this yer granddaughter?"

"No, this here's Maggie Callahan, recently of the settlements. Her and I are travelin' west, lookin' fer her family."

Gimpy nodded. "Kin I offer ya these squirrels?"

Maggie reached up and took them. "Thank you, Mr. Weaver, I'll get these skinned out and roastin' on the fire."

Maggie drew her knife and went to work as the old men settled themselves by the fire.

"Where ya comin' from, Gimp?" Jake asked.

"Jist comin' back from the Ohio Country."

Jake raised his eyebrows. "Don't say? We're headed that way now."

"Yer takin' the Kittanning Road?"

"The same."

"Well, I jist come back that way, you know how to git on the road from here?"

"Not 'zackly," Jake admitted. "I jest figured I'd angle out west of here and hit 'er sooner or later."

Gimpy nodded. "I spec' ya would. But here, I kin show ya a quick way."

Gimpy used his hand to smooth out the dirt by the fire. He picked up a twig and began sketching out a map.

"No special trick to it," he began, "Jist keep down this creekbed, foller that main trail until it turns south then split off west. You'll have to cross these here hills then you'll run dead inta that road. Five, six days of travel and you'll be on the banks o' the Allegheny River, joins with the Ohio further south."

Jake crouched by the fire, making a picture of the map

in his mind.

"And one more thing," Gimpy said, "when ya get to the Allegheny, do yerself a favor. Stop at the tavern by the river and git yerself a good meal."

Jake grinned. "I'll do that, Gimp."

Maggie was spearing the squirrels up on green sticks now and setting them to roast over a low bed of coals.

"Beggin' yer pardon, Miss," Gimpy said, "but I taken notice o' that leather pouch hangin' round yer neck. Are you an herb doctor?"

"No," Maggie said. "There's no herbs in this pouch."

"But it's somethin' jest as healin'," Jake put in.

Gimpy wrinkled his brow. "Hope ya don't mind me bein' curious, but I seen a pouch like that on a woman jist recently." He put his hand to his jaw. "Can't 'member where it was I saw it."

Maggie lifted her pouch up into the firelight. "Inside this pouch is the most precious thing I own," Maggie said, "it's the spook yeast, passed down for seven generations in the Callahan family. It's the sourdough starter we use for bakin' our family bread."

The old man's eye lit up. "Bread, that's it! I seen a pouch like that on a woman's neck out in the Allegheny."

"A bread-baking woman?" she asked.

"Well, sure," Gimpy said, "out there at that tavern I told ya 'bout, on the banks o' the Allegheny."

Jake and Maggie shot a glance at each other.

"What was that woman's name?" Jake asked.

Gimpy closed his eyes, remembering, "Oh, let's see . . . Anna 'er somethin' like that . . ."

"Franny?" Maggie asked.

Gimpy nodded. "Yep, that's it! Franny and her man Thomas. They own that tavern along the road, I had supper with 'em not five nights ago."

Maggie reached over and gripped Jake's hand. "We're gonna find her!" she said. Jake grinned like a possum.

Gimpy frowned. "Well, a'course yer gonna find her, ya couldn't miss the tavern. What do ya think, they put a tavern back in the woods where no one can find it?"

The squirrels were ready now. Maggie was too excited to eat. Her thoughts flew ahead to Franny, on the Allegheny. Her heart lifted, like a sun rising over water.

Jake finished his portion of the squirrel and dropped the bones into the fire, watching the flames turn greasy and blue.

He wiped his mouth with his sleeve. "So, Gimp. You ain't told us where yer headed."

"Up North, placed called New England."

"What business ya got there?"

"I got family there, a sister and I think a brother still alive. I mean to pass out my days on the old family farm."

Jake frowned. "No, Gimp. A true mountain man like you, hoein' corn?"

"Don't mean to hoe no corn. But a body gits to be my age, it's time to quit scramblin' round these mountains. Might fall one day and break a hip. Then where would I be?"

Jake looked into the flames. "Well, Gimp, I spec' yer right."

"This is my last ramble," the older man said, "Mebee you'll understand someday when ya git to be my age, Logan. Time jist creeps up on a man. But enjoy the ramblin' while ya kin, it's the finest pleasure a body kin have, ramblin' the woods, seein' it while it's still wild."

"And now," Gimp said, "now that I've shared yer fire and enjoyed yer hospitality, I'll be movin' along."

"No," Maggie protested, "at least camp here with us for the night."

"No, Miss, yer very kind, but I like travelin' at night. It's cool and quiet and I jist don't seem to need sleep like I usta. Don't worry after me, I'll make out."

The men got to their feet and shook hands across the fire.

"Take care of yerself, Gimp," Jake said.

Gimpy settled his hat on his head. "Yep, be careful yer own self." Then he was gone.

Maggie looked down. "He hardly touched his squirrel."

Jake smiled sadly. "Ya kin have it. Old fella like Gimp, he don't need to eat. Jest lives on sunlight and air and mountain spring water, like an old elm tree."

Jake settled back by the fire, thinking his own thoughts, thinking about time creeping up on a man, and feeling old.

Maggie placed a hand on his shoulder.

"Let's put out the fire and get some sleep," she offered.

Jake shook himself, then brightened. "Tomorrow we got a good day's walk to the road," he said, "but when ya know where yer goin', doesn't seem so far."

Maggie fetched a noggin of water from the creek and

used it to douse the fire. They scattered the ashes in the dark.

Jake felt around for his rifle and hunting pouch.

"Let's find us a rabbit hole," he said.

It was a trick Jake had showed Maggie their first night on the trail.

"If yer travelin' in strange country," Jake had explained, "and ya want ta sleep safe and sound, jest do what the rabbit does: he finds hisself the thorniest, tangliest briar thicket he kin and he climbs right inta the middle of it. He knows that whatever comes sneakin' up on him gotta come through them briars first."

They walked uphill a short distance to a blackberry thicket Jake had noticed while it was still daylight. He went belly-down and snaked his way in among the blackberry canes. Maggie dropped on her hands and knees and followed, bending the canes back into position behind her. They made their leafy beds a few feet apart in the center of the thicket.

Maggie untied her apron and gathered it around her head to keep the bugs off. She lay on her back, letting the drowsiness take her, feeling safe and secure in the circle of the briarwood.

Chapter 2

At first, Maggie wasn't sure what had awakened her. But whatever it was, Jake had heard it too. They both sat up in the chilly dawn air and listened.

Someone was coming on the main trail down by the creekbed. Maggie's first thought was that it might be Gimpy, changing his mind and coming back to join them. She rose to her knees and peered through the tangle of thorns. There was just enough light to make out shapes.

Then Maggie saw them.

"God A'mighty," she whispered, "Indians!"

Jake laid a quieting hand on her shoulder. "Jest set still," he breathed, "mebee they'll pass by."

Maggie could see them coming up into the clearing now, a dozen warriors, some carrying heavy packs. They were heavily armed and dressed for war.

Near the head of the column was one man who attracted Maggie's attention. He was older than the rest and seemed to be the leader.

He was bare-chested, wearing only a loincloth, buckskin leggings and moccasins. But it was his paint that gave him such a shocking appearance: His body was streaked with yellow and green so he blended with the foliage. His face was a mask of black paint. His eyes shone out, sharp and alert, like the eyes of an animal moving through danger. His head was shaved except for a single crowning tuft of hair. In his right hand he carried a short-barreled trade musket. Tucked into his belt was a hatchet, its cutting edge and handle stained with blood.

Then Maggie caught sight of the scalps, dangling from the warriors' belts. They were palm-sized circlets of hair, black and blonde. The blood from the scalps still ran in rivulets down the warriors' naked thighs.

Maggie felt the fear rising in her. She hoped Jake would be right about them passing by. But he wasn't. They dropped their bundles and slumped down to rest, scarcely a stone's throw from where Maggie and Jake hid.

Maggie watched as they took turns drinking spring water and eating stolen bread from the bundles they carried.

Then one of the warriors pointed uphill, toward the

briar patch. He rummaged through the bags and pulled out a pewter teapot.

He walked lazily toward them, the teapot cradled under his arm. He was coming to pick blackberries.

Jake leaned close. "Don't run lest ya have to. We kin still get outa this if we sit tight."

Maggie nodded and crouched low in the briars.

The warrior began picking on the rim of the thicket. But, as always, the best and juiciest berries were in the center. He worked his way through the patch, dropping berries in the teapot as he went. At last he was standing so close to Maggie that she could have reached out and touched his leg.

Suddenly the warrior stopped and peered down through the thicket. He had seen the white of Maggie's apron.

Jake knew the time for hiding was over. He rose straight up through the thicket and swung the barrel of his flintlock, cracking the warrior hard across the ribs. The young man screamed as he collapsed into the thorns.

"Run fer it!" Jake yelled.

Maggie didn't take time to argue, she ripped her way through the thicket and began racing uphill. Before she plunged into the trees, she threw a glance back over her shoulder. She saw Jake, standing up to his armpits in

briars, swinging wildly with his rifle as the warriors drew their tomahawks and waded into the thicket after him.

Maggie hit a deer trail and began to run along the shoulder of the hill. She ran on sheer instinct for a while, then stopped and leaned against a tree to catch her breath. She considered circling back to the clearing to help Jake, but she didn't see how she could. For the moment, it looked as though she had gotten away.

Then she saw him, coming up the trail behind her: a young warrior, his face streaked with blue paint. He had drawn his tomahawk and was quickly closing the distance between them.

Maggie turned to run but tripped over a tree root and fell headlong on the ground. Before she could rise, the warrior was upon her. She drew her sheath knife with her right hand and held up her left to fend off the tomahawk blow.

But it never came. Just as the young man was raising his arm, the war leader came up behind him, grabbed him by the shoulders and threw him to the ground.

Quick as a cat, the blue-faced warrior was on his feet, facing the war leader, his hatchet drawn. The older man still had his hatchet in his belt.

The young man pointed to the scalp at his belt and to Maggie's red hair. He talked hot and fast for several seconds. The older man locked eyes with him for a moment then made a sign with his hand, a sign which, in any language, means: "This conversation is finished." They glared at each other for several moments then the younger man dropped his glance and trotted back to the clearing.

The warrior gestured for Maggie to drop her knife. She let it fall.

He reached into his belt and withdrew a length of strong cord, made from twisted rawhide. One end was formed into a noose. He slipped it over Maggie's head and tightened it snugly around her throat. He paid out four feet of line and looped the other end around his left wrist. He gestured back along the trail, toward the clearing.

Maggie walked ahead the best she could, feeling the cord taut around her neck.

Chapter 3

When they reached the clearing, Maggie didn't expect to find Jake alive. But he was. The young men had taken his weapons and had him seated on the ground, hands tied behind his back, a stick braced in the crook of his elbows.

A short distance away, the warrior Jake had struck with the gun barrel was laid out on the ground, his torso tightly wrapped in canvas. Maggie figured his ribs must be broken.

The warrior glared at Jake. Jake stared straight ahead, his face impassive. Maggie followed the old man's example. She kept her back straight and moved with as much dignity as she could, being led around by a throat-cord.

It was clear to Maggie that as long as she stayed close to the war leader, she was safe from the cruelties of the young men. Jake was not so lucky. As he sat on the ground, the warriors took a delight in poking at him with their feet and tormenting him in small ways. Jake stared straight ahead.

After a few moments, the leader got the war party up and moving again. Maggie was impressed by how quickly they formed up for travel. Ahead, at the point of the line, walked two warriors who served as the eyes and ears of the column. Directly behind them, Maggie and the war leader. Then the burden-carriers, Jake with his broken-ribbed captor, and two heavily armed warriors in the rear. The column moved with astonishing speed and suppleness, like a great silent animal slipping through the woods. Maggie had to walk fast to keep from being pulled by the throat-cord.

Maggie was surprised that the fear hadn't overwhelmed her. Instead, she felt exceptionally alert.

She watched the war leader, walking ahead of her. His eyes were always roving, keeping eye contact with the men ahead and behind, scanning the woods on either side of the trail. Catching the profile of his stern, painted face, Maggie realized it was possible for her to have two conflicting emotions at once.

She felt a hatred and rage toward him because he was the one in control. And strangely, for some reason, she felt grateful to him. For the time being, at least, he had preserved their lives.

Her instincts told her that she must do nothing to show her fear or weakness. And above all, she must prove herself worthy of being kept alive.

That night they camped in a strange place, on the edge of a cliff face which rose forty feet over a large stream. As the war leader tied her cord to a sapling near the edge of the cliff, she saw that a colony of beavers had dammed the stream there, making the deep pool.

The young men dragged Jake to a craggy crab apple tree which stood on the edge of the cliff. There were a few other apple trees around, but this one was different: it was dead and had begun to rot. The beetles had long since worked the bark off and the tree seemed almost white in the twilight.

Maggie watched as they stood Jake up against the tree and bound him to it with wide strips of canvas wrapped round and round his chest. A thought flashed through Maggie's mind: This is a torture tree. She had heard stories about the terrible things that Indians did to their prisoners, now it was happening before her eyes. She knew that Jake's death would take a long time.

She tried to catch Jake's eye, to give him some sort of encouragement, but the old man's face had gone to stone.

Maggie knew that he had gone to a place inside, where the pain could not reach him.

The young men lined up, fifty paces from the tree, and began stringing their bows. The broken-ribbed warrior came forward with an armful of green, wind-fallen apples and began to place them very carefully on Jake's shoulders. The old man held his shoulders square.

When the broken-ribbed one stepped aside, the warriors fitted their arrows to their bowstrings.

Maggie tried to make herself look away, but some strange fascination kept her from doing it. She watched in astonishment as the arrows flew thick and fast around Jake's shoulders, piercing the apples. The old man stood absolutely still as the metal-tipped arrows sunk into the rotten wood around his ears.

Maggie was amazed at the young men's marksmanship. They didn't take time to aim; they simply raised their bows and released. None of the arrows struck Jake. The warrior came forward with another armful of apples, the warriors moved back a few paces.

During the next round, Maggie noticed a few stray shots: one went wild and high, sinking into the wood above Jake's head, the other went low, under his armpit. The metal point of that arrow sliced through the wide canvas band that held the old man to the tree.

Jake felt the binding loosen.

What happened next, happened very fast. Jake threw his full weight against the canvas binding and ripped himself free. He took three running steps and leaped over the edge of the cliff.

The warriors shouted and sprinted to the edge of the cliff, just catching a glimpse of the old man as he disappeared, feet first, into the water. None of the young men dared to jump after him. Instead, they pulled their bows.

Maggie held onto the sapling and looked down over the edge of the cliff. In the failing light, she could make out the ripples made by the swimmer. She watched as the arrows rained down.

The war leader shouted now, pointing to the body floating in the water. The young men circled around and began scrambling and sliding down the cliff to the water's edge.

Maggie watched as a knot of warriors swam out to the body, racing to see who could reach the war trophy first. They converged and lifted the body up out of the water. The young men gave a shout of surprise and disgust. It was not Jake, it was the body of a beaver, with an arrow through its neck.

The war leader shouted down. The men looked up and gestured to their chins then to the white chin marks of the beaver.

Then, Maggie understood: by some strange superstition of war, these young men thought that Jake had changed himself into a beaver.

Chapter 4

It was the day after Jake escaped that Maggie and her captors crossed the West Branch of the Susquehanna River. From there the war party headed north, making over twenty miles a day.

Along the way, Maggie kept close to the war leader and tried her best to keep up. When they made their camps at night, she slept as best she could, tied to a sapling like a dog.

Along the way, she occupied her mind by remembering landmarks. It was a trick Jake had taught her: storing the images of waterways and mountain slopes, an outcrop of rock or a strange-shaped tree by the trail. These would be helpful if she ever got a chance to come back this way.

Maggie thought some about Jake. She decided that he probably hadn't turned into a beaver, as the Indians seemed to believe. The young men had told the story over and over to each other. The war leader had not countered them. Maggie thought he was probably just as glad to be free of the old man.

Maggie decided to let herself think that Jake was still alive and that he had gotten away safely. She decided that it would be too much to ask that he be able to help her in some way. It would be enough, she decided, if the old man was still alive.

After six days of travel, the war party reached the banks of the Genesee river, 200 miles north of Penns Valley.

One day, at about mid-morning, they came to a spot along the river that looked to Maggie like a village.

This had a startling effect upon the warriors: for the first time they seemed to relax, laugh, and talk loudly as they walked. It made Maggie very nervous. There had been a certain security in traveling the war-trail. She had known what to expect and what was expected of her. She had come to believe that if she kept quiet and didn't slow them down, she would be allowed to live. But, up ahead, in the villages, she didn't know what would happen.

The outskirts of the village looked horrible. Along the riverbank stood two crude bark lean-tos.

"Lord," Maggie thought to herself, "could people live in them?"

An old man and a boy came out of the woods and trotted up to the war party. They wore loincloths and tattered cloth shirts.

The old man said a few words to the leader, then led them to a sheltered place along the streambank. Maggie saw what the warriors had come for: five bark-covered canoes, tied to a row of saplings, rode light on the water.

The war party loaded up, two or three men to a canoe, the bundles lashed down. Maggie sat in the war leader's canoe, her in the center, one young man paddling in the bow, the older man in the rear, steering.

Maggie was astonished at the distance they covered in only a few short hours. She watched the muscles ripple on the warrior's back ahead of her. Dip, stroke, glide and swing. Dip, stroke, glide and swing. It was a welcome break from walking.

By noon, they were passing a village. Maggie couldn't see much of it from the river but she knew it was there. The cornfields came right down to the water. She saw the smoke from cooking fires against the sky. She heard dogs barking.

Less than an hour beyond the village, Maggie heard a roaring sound, like distant thunder. The paddlers heard it too. They angled the canoes into shore and began to unload.

Maggie glanced around, confused. There was no village here. Why were they stopping? And what was that sound?

The young men up-ended the canoes and began climbing a well-worn trail along the river bank. Maggie followed along, led by the war leader. As they climbed higher, the air filled with mist. Then she saw and

understood: The river dropped here, a large waterfall and a deep pool below. They carried around the falls, re-packed the gear, and paddled ahead.

In less than a mile they encountered an even bigger falls. This one was over a hundred feet high and was the most majestic Maggie had ever seen. The view from the trail above was breath-taking. From here Maggie could see the wide, deep canyon the Genesee River had cut through rock.

Despite her fear and misery, the physical beauty of the gorge drew her away from her troubles.

Clouds of small birds wheeled and flew up along the cliff walls. Other birds sailed high and majestic, looking for food.

Two hawks glided by, scarcely ten feet away. They flew in tandem, their wings almost touching, cutting the air with a slight sound. Maggie watched the hawks as long as she could. There was something about the ease and grace of their flight that lifted her spirit. She watched them as they spiraled upward on the wind currents, then separated from each other and flew off. Her heart flew with them.

Then they were gone and Maggie was back with her captors on the ground, tethered down by a throat-cord.

They camped that night on the floor of the canyon, by the water's edge. In the morning it took a long time for the sun to reach them, the canyon was so deep. Another morning of dip, stroke, glide and swing.

Near the end of the day, they came upon the war party's home village. Maggie knew this was the end of the journey. She watched as the men re-touched their paint and arranged their clothing. She sat still in the canoe as the leader painted her face bright red and fastened back her hair with a rawhide thong. Maggie looked at her reflection in the water over the side of the canoe. The red paint made her face appear stark and thin, like a deathskull.

They started to come into cornfields then, young corn rising up in the fields on either side of the river bank. She smelled woodsmoke.

The first people she saw were a group of young boys, playing on the rocks by the river. When they got closer, Maggie could see that they were spearing frogs with sharpened sticks.

When the boys saw the canoes approaching, they stood on the rocks and shouted, thrusting their sticks in the air. One of the boys had speared a frog. Maggie watched it kicking, impaled on the wooden point of the spear.

Suddenly, Maggie no longer saw the frog's body, but her own, impaled on the wooden shaft, writhing in pain. All the terrible stories she had heard about Indian tortures began flooding into her mind. Her breathing came in fast, shallow sobs. Up ahead, she could see people coming down to the bank to meet them.

To comfort herself, Maggie reached into her blouse to grasp the pouch of spook yeast. Her fingers groped slowly at first, then frantically.

The pouch was gone!

She searched her clothing and the bottom of the canoe. But it was not there. When had she last seen the pouch? Was it last night, in the camp on the canyon floor? She couldn't remember. It could have fallen away and been lost along the trail anywhere. One thing was clear: her most precious possession was gone.

When Maggie looked up she could see that dozens of Indians had come down to the landing place and were wading out to pull the canoes in. Hands reached out and gripped her by the arms, lifting her up out of the canoe. Somewhere up in the village, she heard drums.

Chapter 5

When they came up through the corn and into the village, Maggie gasped. It was nothing like she had expected. She was prepared to see a cluster of miserable bark huts, like the ones downriver. But this place was different.

The earthen road they walked was a hundred feet wide and ran straight as an arrow to the setting sun in the west. Arranged neatly on either side of the avenue were more than a hundred of the most elegant houses Maggie had ever seen on the frontier. Most were hewn log with shake shingles, but a few were more elaborate, with real glass in the windows.

Each house had a neat yard with vegetables, flowers and fruit trees arranged in orderly rows. In the center of the village was an enormous two-story building of peeled

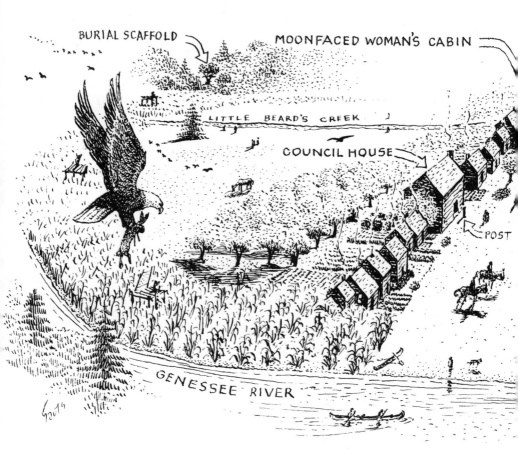

logs, with a red, gabled roof.

A sparkling stream ran through the center of the village. Round and about the town were acres and acres of cornfields, lush grasslands and expansive fruit orchards. It was the most beautiful place she had ever seen.

The people were not at all like she expected either.

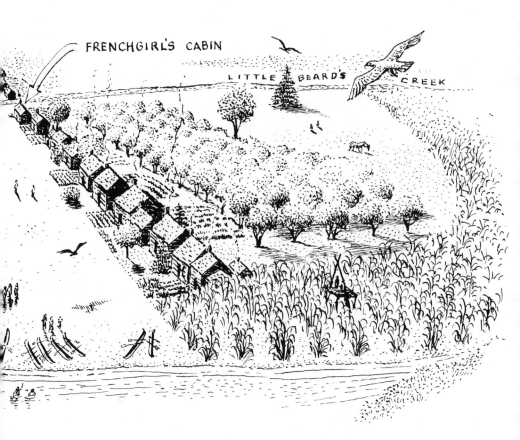

Unlike the warriors, they were dressed in a subtle combination of colonial and native garments. The women wore handsome tradecloth dresses and the men wore colorful shirts and were decked with silver jewelry.

The war leader brought his party up to the red-roofed council house. Sunk into the ground near the doorway was a huge wooden post. The leader pulled his tomahawk from his belt and struck the post. A shout of joy went up from the crowd.

People were coming from all over now: women with babies; children, naked and playful; old men wearing military officer's coats. The drum was still beating somewhere.

The leader raised his hand and the crowd fell silent. He spoke in a rich deep voice for several moments, gesturing toward Maggie and toward the pile of plunder by the war-post.

Maggie was suddenly aware of a large, moon-faced woman standing at her elbow. The woman turned Maggie's face toward her and stared into her eyes.

Although she was trembling inside, Maggie made herself stand with her back straight. She sensed that her fate would be decided within the next few moments.

"Steady now, Maggie," she told herself, "show these people what a Callahan's made of."

The woman stared for a few moments more, then said something to the war leader. For the first time in many days, he slipped the noose from around her neck and tucked it back into his belt.

Then the woman was grabbing her by the wrist and drawing her out of the circle of people. Another woman,

younger but with the same broad features, grasped her other wrist. They held firm to her and brought her down to the stream that ran through the village. They drew her into the water and Maggie watched as they drew their belt knives.

Maggie turned her eyes up to heaven and tried to think of some prayer. She felt the steel blades cutting along her body, cutting away her ragged clothing. The women scooped up handfuls of sand from the creekbottom and rubbed her skin vigorously, washing away the dirt of the war-trail. They washed and plaited her hair then drew her up on the bank and re-touched her face paint.

Back on the shore, they unrolled a bundle, taking out a beautiful tradecloth dress and soft doeskin moccasins.

After she was dressed, the younger woman held Maggie's head firm as the older one pricked a hole through each of Maggie's earlobes. The women worked quickly, running a greased string through each hole.

Then a very strange thing happened. A cluster of women came down to meet them, sobbing as if they were overcome with grief. They led Maggie to a nearby one-room cabin. When they got there, the room was already filled with weeping women. There was not a man in sight.

The moon-faced one began to speak in loud impassioned tones and the wailing grew loud and frightful in

Maggie's ears. She felt afraid for her life and wondered what she could do to defend herself against these women.

The moon-faced woman dried her tears and smiled, placing her hands on Maggie's shoulders. She spoke quietly now. Everyone watched intently as the older woman bent and kissed Maggie on the top of the head.

The women turned and silently filed out, leaving Maggie with her two protectors. They sat Maggie by the fire and gave her a bowl of corn soup. It tasted delicious. Then they showed her to a bed, covered with soft blankets and motioned for her to take off her moccasins and lay down.

Maggie lay there in the dark, listening to the drums and the high-pitched chants outside.

The women murmured softly by the fireplace.

This was a strange place, so much to think about and figure out.

Thought is the enemy of sleep. But sleep is the enemy of thought. The rigors of the war-trail had taken a toll on Maggie's body. She couldn't think anymore. She slept.

Chapter 6

During the first month of Maggie's captivity, her thoughts were filled with plans for escape.

She fell into the rhythm of village life, doing the small household tasks the women allotted to her. But all the while her hands were busy, grinding corn or scraping animal hides, her mind was at work. She noticed everything that went on around her, looking for the hole in the net which would allow her to slip free.

Early on, Maggie realized she had two serious problems.

The first was actually getting away from the village. She was constantly surrounded by people, mostly women. She noticed that these people divided themselves into two broad groups: men and women. Men had their world, outside the village, in warfare, the hunt and diplomacy. Women had their domain in this fertile valley, raising children and food, keeping the households alive and well.

As long as she was within the confines of the town, she knew escape was impossible. But out in the fields, and in the orchards and woods beyond, a person might be able to slip away.

She would wait, she decided, until these people grew confident enough to take her into the fields to hoe corn or into the woods to collect fuelwood. Then she would make her move.

Her second problem was even more troublesome. Once she escaped, where would she go? She thought she might be able to follow the trail back to Penns Valley, but that was a long way and she had already left that place once.

At the heart of it, Maggie realized she needed to push on, west, and find Franny. She tried to picture the map Gimpy Weaver had drawn in the dirt that night. She knew the Allegheny River flowed south along the western border of Pennsylvania, until it joined the Ohio River. That's where Franny was, at Kittanning, on the Allegheny, north of its junction with the Ohio.

But where was the Allegheny in relation to the village? Somewhere off in the west. But how far? She had no idea. There was a blank space in her mental map that had to be filled: the stretch between the Genesee and the Allegheny. For lack of a better plan, she decided to point herself west, hoping to luck onto the river that would carry her home.

A third problem arose, but Maggie pushed it out of her mind as soon as it occurred to her. She didn't want to think about what they would do to her if she were caught.

It was another month before she got her chance to move outside the confines of the town. Maggie could not understand anything of the Seneca language but was made to understand a little of what went on by handsigns and gesture. It was enough.

The moon-faced woman made her to understand that she would be going out to assist in a deer hunt one night in the cedar swamps north of the village. She would help skin and butcher and carry the meat. Maggie did her best to appear indifferent. Inside, she trembled with excitement.

In early evening, Maggie set out by canoe with two men who appeared to be father and son, related in some way to the moon-faced woman. They paddled up a small stream into the thick cedar swamp just as it got dark.

They sat quiet in the canoe for some time before the men struck up a small fire on a flat rock laid across the bow of the canoe. Another flat rock was set up behind it as a reflector. Maggie sat quiet in the center of the canoe. The son knelt with bow and arrows in the bow and the father skillfully steered the craft downstream from the stern.

Then, up on the bank, Maggie saw something: twin points of light, moving in the dark. As they drifted closer, she could see three deer, their eyes shining in the firelight. The deer seemed hypnotized by the light. The canoe drifted close.

At last the young man drew his bow and sent an arrow singing into one of the animals. The deer turned and bolted into the cedars but saw its shadow and leaped back into the water, almost running into the canoe. Maggie watched as the wounded doe bounded up on the opposite bank and fell on its side in the weeds. Meanwhile, the archer had tried a second shot. But the other deer were spooked now and had bounded away into the safety of the swamp.

The father pulled the canoe aside and both men stepped up onto the bank, leaving Maggie behind in the canoe. Maggie hung back.

She watched the men disapper into the brush. She was alone for the first time in weeks.

"This is going to be too easy," she thought to herself. She slipped over the side of the canoe and waded silently into the swamp.

She had no sense of which direction to take but, for now, that didn't matter, what she wanted was to put some

distance between her and the two hunters. She doubted
they could follow her trail through the water.

It was just as she was breaking into the thickest part of
the cedar swamp that she heard them shouting. She could
see their torches bobbing in the dark as they walked up
and down the streamline calling her.

She smiled to herself. She felt as though some of the warrior's stealth on the war-trail had rubbed off on her. She had learned how to travel silently and quietly, even in the dark. Now those skills would be turned in her favor.

By now the swampy water was up to her knees and the bottom of her dress was heavy with water. She considered pulling it up over her head and tossing it aside. But she would need it to protect her from the mosquitos and other biting insects who made the swamp their home. Bugs swarmed around her head and neck. As she had learned on the war-trail, she didn't slap them, that made too much noise. Instead she used the flat of her hand to smear them into her skin.

There was no moon. The night was so dark, the only way for her to steer was to look directly overhead for a space of night sky between the trees. She stumbled on in the blackness. The swamp was fetid here. With each step, she sank deeper into the mud. Swamp gas, smelling like rotten eggs, bubbled up around her legs. The air was hot and heavy with the smell of decayed plant life. The black mud had already sucked one moccasin off her foot. She though she caught another smell, it was the smell of putrefied flesh, an animal that had died there in the swamp. Maggie drew the skining knife they had given her and stepped ahead.

She stepped into a deep hole and went down in the muck, tasting it in her mouth. She dropped her knife. When she tried to wipe her mouth clean, she saw that her hands were covered with the black ooze as well.

Then she caught hold of herself. "Hold up now," she said to herself. "No need to walk anymore, I'll just hold up here until daylight then get my bearings and head south. I left the men far behind."

Maggie found a high piece of ground, big enough for her to lay down on. She pulled the dress over her head and slept like that, off and on, until dawn.

When the first light came into the swamp, Maggie was encouraged. Up ahead, through the trees, she could see a clearing. She thought she must be on the other side of the swamp. She pulled herself to her feet and slipped through the brush, coming out into the clearing. There was a stream here, and a trail, recently traveled. This was a good sign, she thought, this must lead somewhere.

A few steps later she saw a footprint in the mud that looked strangely like her own. Lifting her eyes, her heart sank as she recognized the stream where the deer had been killed the night before.

Sitting under a tree a few feet away, watching her with patient eyes, were the two hunters. She realized she had spent the entire night walking in a great circle through the black cedar swamp.

It was a humiliating feeling to wade up the stream and climb back into the canoe. Her dress was torn and soaked with mud, her arms and legs scratched, one moccasin gone, her face and neck puckered with insect bites.

At that moment, Maggie realized that it wasn't just the Seneca who kept her captive in this valley. Every living thing, down to the smallest insect, conspired against her, keeping her a captive in this strange land.

Chapter 7

Maggie expected some sort of punishment for wandering off into the swamp, but none ever came. The moon-faced woman and her daughter simply cared for her wounds, gave her a new dress and moccasins, and she went back to work. It was a strange way to live, never knowing what was on other people's minds.

It was late summer and Maggie went to the fields every day now, hoeing the weeds back from the tall corn and the bean plants. The soil was rich and black under her bare feet. She worked with the other women, bare-chested in the sun. In the afternoons, they went to the women's swimming place where they shed their clothes and swam in the cool waters of the Genesee before going back to their cabins to prepare the evening meal.

When harvest time came, Maggie was amazed at the

crop: stands of corn with stalks eighteen feet high, ears three feet long and longer, beans that grew long and sweet, squash too big for one person to carry; sunflowers that raised their great faces to the sky.

In October, the Seneca held their annual harvest festival: four days of ceremony, prayers, dancing and music. The village was awake all night, dancing to the heartbeat of the drum. Maggie felt something stir in her. There was something unsettling but beautiful about the high-pitched, wailing chants of the women and insistent beating of drum. She felt on the edge of being swept away by it. But she clung to her own way, drawing back from the dance and the music, as if she were protecting some part of herself.

On the last night of the festival, the moon-faced woman raised her arms and made an announcement to a knot of women standing around her. She gestured toward Maggie as she spoke and then to an old woman who stood nearby; an old crone with a nose hooked down like an owl's beak. In her toothless jaws she clenched a short-stemmed clay pipe. She was beaming with joy. The women smiled at Maggie. She smiled back, uneasily.

The next morning, the moon-faced woman took special care in plaiting Maggie's hair and dressing her in a new tradecloth dress.

"Oh, no," Maggie thought, "whenever they start beauti-fyin' me, I get nervous."

The moon-faced woman took a loaf of cornbread Maggie had baked and placed it in a wooden bowl. She motioned for Maggie to pick up the bowl and follow her down the avenue.

The women of her clan were already waiting outside the cabin. They walked together to a cluster of cabins along the stream, a short distance away. The women there seemed to be expecting her as well. The pipe-smoking matron was there, beaming at Maggie. The moon-faced one motioned for Maggie to hand the cornbread to the older woman. Maggie obeyed. The older woman responded by giving Maggie's family a dried haunch of deer meat. The women gave a joyous shout. Then the crowd fell back, revealing a doorway to one of the cabins.

"Great God," Maggie thought, "am I bein' sold to these people?"

A woman came from the darkness of the cabin, someone Maggie hadn't noticed before. She was different from the others — dressed Seneca but with hair as blonde as corn silk and skin light like Maggie's. In the crook of her left arm, she held a tiny infant wrapped in rabbitskin.

The woman extended her right hand. "Come in, Redwing, I've been waiting for you."

There was a little of the French lilt in her voice, but
Maggie understood the words clearly. It was the first
English she had heard spoken in three months.

Maggie took the woman's hand and stepped over the
doorsill into the cabin.

It was dark and took a moment for her eyes to adjust to
the light. The first thing she noticed were the smells:

Pungent and rich but not unpleasant. Then she saw —
bundles of herbs hung drying from the rafters overhead.
She recognized sassafras roots and the leaves of the
horsemint but the others were strange and unknown to
her. She smelled the woodsmoke from the fireplace and
the milky-sweet fragrance of the baby.

"This will be your home now. We will share the work,
eh?" the woman said.

"Thank you," Maggie said, not quite sure what she was
thanking her for. It felt very good to hear something in her
own language.

"I am Frenchgirl — that is what the English call me.
Until you learn the Seneca, I will help you along in
English."

"When were you captured?" Maggie asked.

Frenchgirl laughed. "A very long time ago, when I was
very small. My father was a fur trader, of the French. My
mother was English. But now I am Seneca."

Maggie shook her head. "But how can that be?"

"I was adopted, just as you have been. And to the
Seneca, I am as much a relative as if I had been born here.
It is the same with you."

"I see," Maggie said slowly. "And the name you called
me — what is it?"

"Redwing. That is the English for your Seneca name.

But listen, my girl is falling asleep. Let me put her to bed and we can sit by the fire and string beans, we will talk as we work, eh?"

Maggie nodded and watched as Frenchgirl tenderly laid her baby on one of the beds.

She glanced around the cabin. She could see much more clearly now. It was well-repaired and everything was in order. Along both sidewalls she could see platform beds, piled high with woolen blankets and warm winter furs. There was a fine stone fireplace with iron pots and kettles, wooden spoons and drinking cups. Thick rawhide, stretched drum-tight over the window frames, let in a warm yellow light.

Frenchgirl brought a birch-bark basket of string beans, needles and thread. They began to string the beans into a long chain to be hung from the rafters to dry.

"When you came to this village," Frenchgirl began, "you were adopted by the Turtle Clan women to replace someone they had lost last year — a young man who died on the war trail. They gave you a new life then — as a Seneca. With a new name: Redwing, for the red of your hair, so much like the feathers of a songbird that catch the sunlight."

Maggie said she understood. They talked. They talked for hours, stringing beans. After a while, Maggie forgot she was deep in Indian country, far from home. For that afternoon, it seemed to her that they could have been two young women anywhere, sitting by the fire, working and talking.

The next morning, they worked outside in the brisk autumn air, pounding corn with the mortar and pestle which stood outside the cabin door.

As they worked, Frenchgirl smiled. "You haven't asked about my brother. Are you shy about asking?"

Maggie wasn't aware she had a brother. But, eager for any kind of conversation, she simply nodded. "Tell me about him."

Frenchgirl wrinkled her brow. "You don't sound very curious."

"No," Maggie said, not wanting to offend, "tell me everything."

Frenchgirl smiled and went back to pounding corn. "That's more like it!"

"He is a runner, a messenger, who carries dispatches from one end of the Iroquois country to another. He is called Firefly. That would be his English name.

"He runs with my husband, Cornstalk. They run together, as a team. They travel light and move very fast. They will be returning soon."

Frenchgirl paused.

"Good," Maggie said absently.

Frenchgirl laid her wooden pestle aside. "Redwing, is there no blood in your veins?"

Maggie continued pounding, "I don't understand."

"You don't seem anxious to meet my brother."

"Not to cause offense, but why should I be?"

Frenchgirl wrinkled her brow. "You might take an interest in him, now that he is your husband . . ."

Maggie stopped the corn pestle in mid-air. "My husband? I don't have a husband."

"Of course you do. Why do you think you came to live with me? Surely you knew. Or at least you expected — the announcement and the ceremony yesterday morning — the exchanging of gifts. What did you think was happening?"

"I thought I was being sold," Maggie answered.

Frenchgirl threw her head back and laughed. "A Seneca woman can't be sold!"

Maggie felt the ire rising in her. "Well how was I to know that? How am I to know anything? I haven't understood anything for a long time —" She felt tears of frustration welling up in her eyes. "Look," she said slowly, "you can explain this to them. You can make them understand. They will see that it was all a mistake and that I didn't give my consent. Besides," Maggie laughed, "I can't possibly be married. I don't even know your brother."

Frenchgirl shook her head gravely. "That does not matter. I didn't know my husband before we were married either. Here the marriages are arranged by the mothers. But they make a good match. I assure you, you will be pleased."

"And if I refuse?"

"Redwing, don't make life hard for yourself and others. Don't shame the ones who have planned so well for you."

Maggie felt her anger erupting. "I don't want anything planned for me —"

"But Redwing —"

"And stop calling me that name!" Maggie shouted. "My rightful name is Maggie. I am a Callahan, I'm Irish. I was born that way, I will die that way!"

Frenchgirl shook her head patiently. "No, Redwing, you are wrong. This Maggie person you speak of — she is dead. The women of the clan could have taken your life. But they didn't, they decided to spare you and give you a new life — as a Seneca. Do not throw your life away foolishly."

As Frenchgirl's words sunk in, Maggie flashed back to the horror and fear she had felt back on the war-trail. She knew that Frenchgirl was right, they could have taken her life. But she was alive.

"Our men will return in a few days. They are now to the east, on a war party," Frenchgirl explained. "When they return the season for war will be over and we will leave for the winter elk hunt."

"We will pack a canoe and go south, to the river the English call the Allegheny. Do you know of this river?"

The Allegheny! This was the missing link! Maggie tried to make her voice sound calm. "I have heard the name, that's all," she said.

They worked quietly then, Maggie's mind racing through the possibilities. Now, her escape plans fell together quickly. She would go with this hunting party, allowing them to escort her out of the village and across the wild unknown terrain until they reached the Allegheny. It would be much easier to slip away from them if she appeared to enjoy the trip.

"All right," Maggie thought, "I will marry this man, this Firefly. I will become the model Seneca wife for a week or two. Then — gone, gone home to Franny and my own people."

Maggie went about her work smiling when she could, scarcely able to sleep at night, working in the day with an eye toward the main road, waiting for her husband to arrive.

Chapter 8

Maggie and Frenchgirl were up in the hills collecting firewood the afternoon their husbands came in.

When the women returned to the cabin, they saw two blanketed forms, rolled up by the fire, fast asleep.

Frenchgirl clucked her tongue. "The men. I wish they'd learn to use the beds. They are used to sleeping on the ground by the fire, eh?" Then she smiled.

"What should we do?" Maggie asked. Her hands were shaking as she stacked the firewood in the corner.

Frenchgirl took her baby out of the backsling and placed her on the bed. "We will take care of their feet, now. That is the first thing. Then we will take care of the rest of them." Frenchgirl brought a kettle of water and a wooden bowl, filled with clean rags.

"They may not wake at first," Frenchgirl explained.

"They have been running for two days, coming from the Mohawk country in the east."

Maggie was amazed. "Two days? But the Mohawks must be 150 miles from here. No one can run 150 miles in two days. It can't be done."

Frenchgirl nodded. "I know. But they do it anyway. Wait until you see their feet."

Maggie looked at the dark forms huddled by the fire. "Which one is mine?"

Frenchgirl nodded to the one lying on his back by the fire. "That one."

Maggie crept up to him in the dim light and began unwrapping the blanket strips wrapped from the knee to the ankle on his lower legs. Underneath, she could see that the buckskin leggings were wet from dashing through streams.

"They're soaking wet," Maggie whispered, "How do they keep their feet from freezing?"

Frenchgirl smiled faintly. "They keep moving."

Now Maggie watched as Frenchgirl drew her knife and cut the frozen laces, easing off her husband's thick elkhide over-moccasins. She did the same. Maggie was shocked to see that both men's feet were wrapped in bloody rags. The women unwound the rags and pulled the cloth away from the skin. Maggie could see the horrible toll the constant running had taken on the men's feet.

"They will heal," Frenchgirl assured her, "I've seen them worse than this." They washed the men's feet and wrapped them in clean rags.

It was during the foot-washing that the two husbands began to stir under their blankets. Out of the corner of her eye, Maggie could see her man sit up. It seemed an incredibly long time before she could make herself turn her head and look into her husband's eyes.

He was not at all as she had expected. His features were not the strong ones of the Indian men she had seen, instead they were finely etched, almost delicate. He wore his blonde hair long, in a scalplock that trailed down his back. His eyes were a piercing blue and he had one tattoo: A series of tiny deer tracks that led from the outside corner of his right eye to the right-hand corner of his mouth. For a moment she was lost in the blue of his eyes, then she made herself look away.

Frenchgirl's husband sat up then and she placed her baby on Cornstalk's lap. He lifted the child up overhead and laughed softly. Like Firefly, he wore his hair in a scalp-lock. He was larger, but he still had a runner's lithe form.

Maggie was momentarily thrown off guard. She had expected these trail-hardened men to stride into the cabin full of pomp and bloodlust. Instead, they seemed almost shy in the women's presence.

After the women had served up some corn soup, Frenchgirl whispered, "Well, what do you say Redwing?"

Maggie shook her head. "Your brother, he is so quiet."

"Ah," Frenchgirl nodded. "You must understand, these men live by quiet. It is what saved their lives. They are fierce and quiet on the war-trail, gentle at home. In some things," she said significantly, "the women must take the lead."

That night Maggie lay in her bed listening to Frenchgirl and her husband laughing and cooing with their baby in the bed against the opposite wall. Firefly slept rolled in his blanket by the fire. Maggie lay awake most of the night, turning things over in her mind. But she was the only one awake. Everyone else slept soundly.

The next morning Frenchgirl said, "Today you will learn to make moccasins. You are a runner's wife. You will make many pairs and you must be able to do it well. On the trail, our men's well-being often depends upon the condition of their feet, eh?"

Frenchgirl showed Maggie how to measure the men's feet and how to use an old moccasin as a pattern. They worked as long as the light was good, making three pairs each.

"There," Frenchgirl said when they had finished, "That is the last of the elkhide. But we will have more soon."

"When do we leave for the hunt?"

"When the men's feet are healed. Maybe ten days. It is late in the season to start. Most of the families have left on the hunt already. But there is nothing to be gained by hurrying."

It was late in November when they left for the elk hunt. Frenchgirl left her child with one of the clan women. The woman held the baby up high until the canoe disappeared down the stream. "Goodbye, village," Maggie thought, knowing that each paddle-stroke was bringing her closer to Franny and freedom.

It was three days of hard travel and makeshift camps until they reached the headwaters of the Allegheny river. Eighty miles south of the village, Maggie realized she could have never made the journey by herself.

Once on the Allegheny, Frenchgirl and Maggie set up a camp on a large island in the middle of the river.

"We will flesh the hides and dry the meat here," Frenchgirl explained. "There is much to do but it is happy work. We can dry enough meat for the whole winter during this trip. This is a good camp. On this island, we won't have to worry about animals."

"What animals?" Maggie asked.

"In this country, there are many animals that would come to steal the meat from our racks: small ones like raccoons and squirrels, big ones like bears and wolves."

"Wolves?" Maggie said.

Frenchgirl nodded toward the riverbank. "They are up there. They hunt the deer, as we do, killing the old and sick and some young."

"That seems cruel of them," Maggie remarked. Frenchgirl shook her head. "Not at all. In this way, the wolves make the elk strong by assuring that only the healthiest survive. In this way, with each kill the wolf assures that the next generation of elk will be just as strong. Our men do that when they hunt. In this way the wolf and the man are the same."

"But aren't the men afraid of the wolves? The wolves can hunt men as well," Maggie asserted.

"No," Frenchgirl said. "This is not so. A wolf would have to be very hungry to attack a man."

Maggie turned that over in her mind. "I see."

The men spent the first day scouting the shoreline in the canoe. The women set up camp and made corn soup. That night the men sat up by the fire.

Maggie went down to the water's edge to carry back some water. It was dark now but the moon was full and bright, giving the water and the land beyond it a ghostly light. As Maggie was dipping her bucket, she heard a sound coming out across the water. It was a beautiful liquid sound, something like the call of a bird. But Maggie didn't think it was a bird. It was much too complex and ever-changing to be simply an animal call. It was plaintive and at the same time peaceful, filled with longing and sadness. Maggie listened until it was over, then turned and hurried up the trail toward the camp.

"I heard this sound, down by the water," Maggie told Frenchgirl.

She didn't see Frenchgirl smile in the darkness.

"I didn't hear anything," she said.

The next morning, when Maggie unrolled her blanket by the fire, she could see that Frenchgirl, Cornstalk, and the canoe were gone. Firefly sat in his blanket by the fire, staring out across the water.

Maggie rose and pulled on her moccasins, went down to the river's edge and washed her face and hands in the cold water. Then she came back to the fire and warmed her palms. She nodded to Firefly. He nodded back shyly.

Maggie thought to try some sign language. She pointed to where the canoe had been tied up by the bank then shrugged.

Firefly understood. He made a sign for shooting a rifle then spread his fingers atop his head for the antlers of the elk.

"Gone hunting," Maggie muttered to herself.

She pointed to the sun overhead and shrugged. "How long?" she asked.

Firefly seemed eager to communicate, even in this simple way. He held up four fingers.

"Ah," Maggie thought, "four hours." She made the handsign which brought the sun to noon.

Firefly shook his head. He pointed to the sun and brought it around four times.

Maggie had a sinking feeling. "Four days?"

Maggie didn't think it was going to be like this. Four days alone on the island with a man she hardly knew. What would they do in all that time? Maggie made some hot water and they drank a cup of tea, each, staring out at the grey, cold waters. Then they had a biscuit and another cup of tea, each.

Maggie had an inspiration. She pointed to the firewood pile and to the handaxe stuck in a log nearby. "We will collect firewood," she thought to herself, "make ourselves useful."

He picked up his axe and headed away from camp. Maggie realized he was as uncomfortable as she was.

They worked all that afternoon, bringing in the wood. Late in the day, she sighed to herself, "If I don't think of somethin' else to do, there won't be a stick of firewood left on this island." She decided to cook something. She made some corncakes in the ashes of the fire. They ate their meal, avoiding each other's eyes. Darkness came early and the cold clamped down over the water. They built the fire big and watched the cold moon come up.

Firefly rose and wrapped his blanket around him, shaking his legs, stiff from cold. Then he walked off into the woods.

Maggie stared into the fire. A moment later she heard that bird-like sound, the musical sound she had heard the night before. She ventured away from the warmth of the fire, following the sound which seemed to be coming from the river itself.

She felt drawn to it in some strange way. The sadness of the melody tugged at her heart, reaching back into the loneliness of her own heart.

Then she saw Firefly, sitting on a tree trunk along the water's edge. Perhaps he had heard the sound too. As she came closer she could see that the sound was coming from him.

It wasn't until she was perhaps six feet away that she could see how the music was made. Firefly was playing a long wooden flute, not blowing sideways like the Irish flutes, but blowing into the end and fingering the tunes

with a series of noteholes. It was impossible for Maggie to tell how long she stood listening to the music before she crept up and sat beside him on the log. But the flute had done its work.

It is not important, or even possible, to tell everything that happened to Maggie that night, or in the next three days on the island.

It is enough to say that they learned to talk in handsigns. They swam in the icy moonlit water and ran laughing to the fire where they huddled in warm bearskin robes. They cooed and laughed and held each other under the great star-sprinkled night and listened to the sound of the water lapping up on the shores of their tiny island camp.

It is enough to say that, for the first time in her life, Maggie knew what it was to fling herself away, out of her body, and to feel at one with the earth and the water and the stars overhead.

Chapter 9

Maggie and Firefly saw the canoe coming from a long way off, gliding across the cold waters to their warm island camp.

When Frenchgirl and Cornstalk pulled their craft up along the landing place, Maggie could see that the canoe was riding low with the weight of a huge elk. Frenchgirl had taken off the skin and antlers and quartered the carcass to make it easy to carry.

Firefly waded down into the shallows and pulled the loaded canoe up to shore. Cornstalk was happy as only a hunter can be happy.

Frenchgirl was happy as well. She grasped Maggie's arm and stepped up onto the bank. "I'm glad things went so well for you and Firefly," she said.

Maggie pursed her lips playfully. "Why are you so sure

things went well with us?"

Frenchgirl threw her head back and laughed. "Are you serious? It is written on your face. And we could tell from a great distance offshore. The two of you — your mouths were smiling and your eyes were smiling, your whole bodies were smiling."

Maggie felt the color rising in her face.

"Is it that obvious?"

Frenchgirl grinned, "It is nothing to be embarrassed about, Redwing. The flute has great power, no?"

They laughed. It was the laughter that only two married women can share.

It was hard work the rest of the day, but it was happy work. It was the work of plentifulness. Frenchgirl showed Maggie how to slice the meat into thin strips and lay it out on the wooden drying rack by the fire. They stretched the huge skin out between two trees, to dry in the open air.

Meanwhile the men carefully removed the sinew from the legs and from both sides of the backbone. This would be bowstrings and sewing thread, Frenchgirl explained.

Maggie noticed that there was a use for every part.

"It is our obligation to the elk, to use every part we can. This way the spirit of the deer will be pleased and we will have good hunting another time," Frenchgirl explained.

That night they feasted on the fresh liver. They laughed a lot by the fire that night. When they rolled in their warm bearskins and watched the stars wheel and spin in the cold clear sky overhead, Maggie found herself wishing that this hunting trip would never end. It snowed that night.

For days after that, they fell into a routine: The men went hunting morning and evenings and the women worked at scraping the hides and drying the meat during the days. Cornstalk said that Firefly would be no good for the hunt after the time he had spent with Maggie. Firefly knew it brought bad luck on a hunter to have such close contact with his wife while hunting.

One afternoon, Cornstalk trailed single-handedly and killed a huge elk up in the woods, about a half mile from the water's edge. He gutted the animal out and covered it with leaves to hide it from other animals then set out for the island camp to get help in packing the huge carcass down to the water.

The band of four was overjoyed when Cornstalk showed them the body of the huge elk up in the woods. It would take several trips to load it into the canoe.

They first rolled the animal on its back and skinned off the hide. Then Maggie helped as they took their axes and chopped through the backbone, dividing the huge carcass into sections that could be easily carried.

Frenchgirl laid the hide out on the snowy ground and piled the liver, heart, pancreas, stomach on it so they would stay clean. She rolled the hide up.

"Cornstalk and I will take the canoe," Frenchgirl told Maggie. "It will take several loads to bring the elk down to the water. You and Firefly will begin the work of carrying the meat down to the water's edge. It will be hard work."

"We don't mind," Maggie assured her.

"Good," Frenchgirl answered. "We will take the first load across now and come back for a second as soon as we can."

They had plenty of light for the first trip down and they carried the hide and a fair amount of meat because there were four of them then. But Maggie knew they must make at least one more trip back. It would be just Firefly and herself that time and it would be getting dark. But they could easily follow their trail in the light dusting of snow and once the moon came up, there would be enough light.

It was dark by the time she and Firefly reached the water's edge with the last load of meat. They piled the butchered carcass on a rock and stood waiting for the canoe.

Maggie noticed that it had gotten quite cold after the sun went down. She hadn't noticed it while they were working, but now that they had stopped, their clothes moist with sweat, she began to feel a chill creeping through her. Firefly began to shiver too. They danced around in the snow, laughing, to keep the blood circulating through their limbs. But after a while, even that wasn't sufficient. Maggie wanted a fire, but knew they couldn't have one. She knew the smell would alert the animals and ruin the hunting along that side of the river. She certainly didn't want to do that.

Maggie watched Firefly, hopping up and down on the balls of his feet, eyes scanning the water. It was dark and there wasn't much you could see. Where were they? And why were they taking so long? They should have been back long before now.

Maggie touched Firefly on the arm and pointed to her feet. She felt them beginning to freeze. Firefly nodded. He looked about them for a sheltered place to get out of the cold. Then his eyes fell on the elkhide, rolled up and sitting atop the rock. He quickly went to it, unrolled it and piled the organs with the other meat.

Maggie watched as he laid the hide down on the snow, hair side up. He drew her over and laid her down lengthwise on the hide. Then he laid beside her and she turned with him as they rolled up in the hide. It was a good idea. The thick winter coat of the elk made a warm, luxurious nest. In a short time the combination of their body heat and the protection of the elkhide made them tolerably warm.

Once the blood returned to her freezing limbs, Maggie felt a pleasant drowsiness. Both she and Firefly dozed off, secure that they could stay this way until their companions arrived. They were careful to keep their feet well covered at the tail end of the hide but left their faces protruding through the upper end of the roll so their breath wouldn't mist and soak the hairs around them.

It was hours later, well into the night, that Maggie was awakened by a sound nearby. She came to consciousness slowly, reluctant to come out of her warm sleep. She glanced around the clearing. The moon had dipped low now and made eerie shadows on the snow. But something was moving over by the pile of meat on the rock. She saw the sparkling of a dozen pairs of eyes. She squinted, trying to make out the dark shapes. Then she knew them for what they were — wolves!

The sounds she heard were the snufflings and scratching and growls of the wolves as they tore into the frozen carcass of the elk, barely thirty feet from where she and Firefly lay.

Maggie saw that Firefly was awake as well. Knowing they could not speak, Maggie quickly considered what they could do. They had their skinning knives and hand-axes in their belts, so they had weapons. But lying on the ground as they were, they were vulnerable. Ever so slowly, Maggie felt Firefly beginning to sit up. She knew what they must do and she knew they must do it together. They would roll out of the hide, get to their feet and draw their axes. Maggie scanned the clearing for a tree to climb. It would have to be done smoothly and quietly. The wolves would be surprised, Maggie was counting on that.

Maggie tried to raise her arms but found she could not. She flexed her feet but found they were bound as well. She noticed that Firefly was having trouble moving as well. She struggled harder. She was wrapped tight in the hide.

Then she realized what had happened: In the terrible cold, the elkhide had frozen solid around them, holding them tight like a sheath of iron.

The noise they had made in struggling inside the hide
had attracted the attention of the wolves. The animals
hunched their backs and growled. A few of the bolder
ones began to venture toward the hide. Maggie held as
still as she could.

Then she heard the scratching of the wolves' claws on
the hide and heard them growling as they used their teeth

to pull the scrappy pieces of meat off the outside of the skin. One of the wolves cautiously leaped on top of the roll and Maggie could feel its weight on her legs. Then she heard a tearing sound. They were ripping through the hide around their legs!

All at once, Firefly began singing a loud chant. Maggie began singing as well. The noise frightened the wolves and they retreated, dancing away a few steps through the snow. Maggie noticed that one of the bigger animals had something in its mouth. The wolf dropped it on the ground in front of him and the other wolves made a grab for it. But the large wolf picked it up and trotted off into the woods with it. Maggie had seen what it was: It was one of Firefly's moccasins.

Maggie knew the wolves must have torn through the hide and pulled the moccasin off his foot. But the singing had scared them away, for the moment.

Maggie felt a draft of cold air coming up her legs from the hole in the hide.

They sang as loudly as they could and the wolves seemed to back off, clustering around the meat on the rock and watching with glowing eyes.

Then Maggie heard a rifle shot out across the water. She knew Cornstalk must be signalling. The wolves stood still. The shot had frightened them but not enough to run them off. Would they stay and make a stand over the meat?

Then Maggie heard Cornstalk's voice shouting. Maggie craned her neck and could see the canoe, standing in the shallows. She was surprised that Firefly didn't answer. When she turned to look at him, he appeared to be asleep. He had stopped singing.

"Frenchgirl, can ya hear me?" Maggie shouted.

"Where are you?" Frenchgirl shouted back.

"We're on the ground, by the big rock with the meat on it."

Frenchgirl shouted, "We can see the wolves. Don't worry about the meat, Redwing. Cornstalk has his rifle. Just make a run for the canoe, the two of you."

"We can't move. We're frozen into this hide."

Maggie heard Cornstalk and Frenchgirl talking in the canoe.

"All right," Frenchgirl said at last. "Get ready. We are coming in."

Maggie watched as Frenchgirl lit up a torch from a pine knot. They stepped ashore. Maggie could see that French-girl held the torch in one hand and her short-handled axe in the other. Cornstalk held the rifle ready as they slipped across the snow between Maggie and the wolves. Maggie knew that at any moment the wolves might try to rush them. She knew that there would be no way she could help fight them off. But the wolves simply stood their ground. Frenchgirl slipped up and used her knife to saw through the hide.

The wolves watched with glowing eyes.

"If you feel the blade of the knife come near you, tell me," Frenchgirl breathed.

It took a long time to saw through the layers of thick frozen hide and to peel it back from their bodies. Maggie sat up and looked at the bottom of the elkhide. It had been chewed to pieces and was drenched with blood.

"Don't look down there," Frenchgirl said sharply.

But it was too late. Maggie had already seen it. She caught a glimpse of Firefly's exposed ankle in the moonlight. She saw the white bone and sinew and the blood that looked black on the snow. She knew that when the wolf had carried away Firefly's moccasin, his foot had been inside it.

"He's lost a lot of blood," Frenchgirl said simply. She was using a rawhide thong to tie off the wound, staunching the flow of lifeblood.

The wolves did not fight. As Cornstalk stood staring them down with his rifle, Maggie and Frenchgirl carried Firefly to the canoe. It was hard work getting his limp body into the craft. Frenchgirl called to Cornstalk and he backed down away from the cluster of wolves and stepped into the canoe. The wolves turned back to their meat.

Maggie didn't remember much about the rest of the night. Somehow they must have made the paddle back to the island and gotten Firefly up into their makeshift shelter. She felt very tired that night but couldn't sleep. She sat up by the dying fire, holding her husband's head in her lap, listening to his breathing ebb and flow. Sometimes it sounded like the water coming in.

The next morning Frenchgirl told Maggie:

"We will leave now, head back to the village. We will have to leave the meat behind so my brother has room to lie down in the canoe. You will take his place at the paddle. It will be a hard trip back. The water is already freezing in some of the smaller streams. We will have a lot to carry over the portages. Can you do it?"

Maggie took a long time in answering. She knew now that it would not be so hard to steal the canoe and head south, downriver. But she knew that was not right.

"I will do it," she said simply.

Frenchgirl nodded. "Good. I knew you were a Seneca."

Chapter 10

Firefly did not live long. He managed to hang on to life for a little over a month after they returned to the village. In all that time, he never regained consciousness.

Maggie felt a strange and unexplainable longing for this man she had loved, but scarcely known.

Frenchgirl, torn by her own grief, explained what they must do to make sure Firefly would reach the hereafter.

"He was a Seneca," she said softly the afternoon he died. "We'll follow the Seneca tradition. The old people say that it takes one year for the dead to make the journey to the land of the creator."

"The happy hunting ground?" Maggie asked, trying to understand.

Frenchgirl smiled, "No, that is not our name for it. Hunting, as you know, is hard and dangerous work. In this place there is no danger or pain, families are reunited and live in harmony.

"After a year has passed, we will release a bird in Firefly's name. That bird will carry his spirit to the creator. Then we will exchange our sadness for rejoicing because we will know that Firefly is safe. In the meantime, there is much for you and I to do."

"We will bury him?" Maggie asked.

"No, we won't close him up in the ground. We will build a bark platform and set it up in the branches of a tree out from the village. We will lay his remains in that tree where the sun can shine on them and where the wind and rains can wash his bones clean.

"In the meantime, we must make sure that Firefly has all he needs for the journey to the spirit world. We will lay his hatchet and skinning knife beside him, a pipe and some tobacco. We will make sure that he is dressed properly. We will make sure that he has food for the journey. And we must go out to the burial scaffold each night and kindle a fire so that he can prepare his evening meal. If you feel you can't do this, ask me and I will do it."

Maggie shook her head. "No, I will do it."

So this became a small ritual for Maggie. Every evening, just at twilight through the rest of the winter, Maggie made her way out to the tree where Firefly lay and struck up a flint and steel fire in a circle of rocks by the base of the tree.

Sometimes she sat by the fire and wept. Sometimes she spoke out loud to Firefly, knowing there was no one else to hear. The fire itself made her sad. If only she had insisted on a fire that night along the Allegheny. The fire would have kept the wolves away and all this might not have happened.

Maggie lost her desire to eat. She felt sick. One night, late in winter, she was sitting by the fire at Firefly's tree when she saw something moving out across the snow, perhaps a hundred yards away. Even though it was dark, the starlight and the snow made it easy to see the figure. Maggie watched curiously. Who could be out at this time of night in this cold weather?

Whoever it was, they were poking around with a long stick down by the garbage dumps. This is where the village people came to heap up all their trash: Broken pottery and torn clothing, the rotted and frozen carcasses of meat and vegetables that had gone bad. Even in cold weather, a powerful stench came up from that area. The village dogs ran wild down there. But as Maggie watched, the ragged figure pointed its staff and the dogs stepped back and fell silent. Maggie watched until she couldn't see the figure any more.

On several other nights, she caught glimpses of this mysterious person, picking through the dumps. One night, after Maggie returned, she asked Frenchgirl about it.

"Ah," Frenchgirl said, "That is the Rag-Picker. She is an old woman who lives in the thicket down by the garbage heap."

"Why do you call her that?"

"She lives by picking through the garbage, she lives by wearing the clothes and eating the food that someone else had thrown away."

"But why? The other old people in the village have all they need to eat and wear, they have a place to live. I can see that with my own eyes."

"Yes," Frenchgirl said, "what you say is true. And I suppose she could claim her right if that is what she wanted. But she does not. She prefers to live on garbage rather than ask for another's help."

"But her family —"

"She has no family. At least not in this village. No one knows where she came from. Some of the women say that she is a witch and she was banished from her own village."

"A witch?"

"Of course, you have heard stories of people who have the power to cast spells, to kill with a glance, to make animals and plants sicken and die?"

Maggie nodded. "Of course, but those are just wild stories. You don't believe them, do you?"

"I don't know for sure. I think she is simply an old woman. Maybe she had a dream about this way of life. But there is one puzzling piece to the story which I do know."

"Tell it, then."

"Well, one evening, a child died mysteriously. It was a child who had been playing down by the dump. The parents were sure that the Rag-Picker had killed the little girl. So a knot of people went down there the next morning, to hunt her down and kill her. But she had vanished. They could find no sign of her. They searched for weeks but they never found her hut or even her tracks. Very mysterious. People have caught glimpses of her, now and then, but no one has ever seen her up close. Some say she has magical powers, but I don't know."

Suddenly Maggie remembered how she had seen the old woman point her staff at the dogs, how they had fallen silent and backed away.

After that, Maggie kept an eye out for the Rag-Picker each night as she walked to the burial scaffold. She felt strangely repelled, but at the same time, attracted by this old woman.

One night, leaving the burial fire of her husband, Maggie walked out across the snow, down to the dump. It was a clear, cold night and she could easily make out tracks in the snow. Many were the tracks of people who came during the day to cast their offal into the stinking piles. But there was one set of tracks — small moccasin prints with sharply pointed toes that seemed to lead off into another direction, into the thicket away from the village.

Maggie crept into the forest of thin saplings. There was a rude path that wound down through the thicket and fell down along a stream that ran gurgling through the snow. Maggie smelled woodsmoke. Moving as slowly as she could, she urged herself on through the trees, numbed by fear and driven on by an unexplainable urge to find out about this mystery.

Then, up ahead, Maggie saw a tiny flickering fire. There was no sign of the old woman but Maggie could make out the outlines of the hut. It was a small, conical dwelling, made from a framework of branches, piled high with hides and rags and an accumulation of years of filth and dirt. The roof of the hut was overgrown with roots and dead vines that poked up through the snow. The camp smelled like rotted garbage.

Then Maggie saw the Rag-Picker. She emerged from the hut carrying an armful of small objects. The old woman set her bundles on a blanket by the fire.

In the firelight, Maggie could see the old woman clearly. She was hideous: dressed head to foot in layers of filthy and ragged clothing, a mixture of hides and moth-eaten wool. Her hair was black as the night, but streaked with gray and white in places. On her feet were misshapen moccasins which came to a sharp point at the toe. The only bits of her skin exposed to the light were her hands, which looked like the gnarled claws of a bird. Her face was as creased and wrinkled as an apple left to sour on the tree. Her eyes picked up the firelight like a wild animal's.

Maggie watched as this fantastical woman fumbled through her bundles. She took out seven corn-husk dolls, like the ones the little girls in the village played with. Each doll was about as long as the woman's forearm. They had no faces but were dressed carefully in clothing made from scraps of hide and cloth which had come from the dump.

Maggie watched, fascinated, as the Rag-Picker boiled some corn soup in a pot on the fire then spooned out a small portion to each doll, serving them in bowls made from broken pieces of crockery. The old woman muttered and clucked lovingly to each doll as she used her horn spoon to lift the corn soup to their featureless faces, then wiped their mouths clean with a bit of filthy rag.

After the old woman had fed her family of dolls, she took each one to her withered breast and nursed it, singing a pretty sort of lullaby in an old cracked voice. Then the woman carried her tiny family inside and slid the door flap closed.

Maggie backed out of the thicket, trying to wipe her tracks out with a branch. Surely the woman would know

she had been there. She felt as though she had taken an awful chance but that, on some deep and unexplainable level, it had been worth it.

When she arrived at the cabin late that night, Frenchgirl helped her out of her frozen clothing.

"I was worried for you," she said, "where have you been all this time?"

Maggie decided that this was not something she was ready to tell, even to Frenchgirl. "Just walking," she said.

Frenchgirl took Maggie's hands and drew her over to the hearthfire. "You are not well, Redwing. Perhaps you should let me carry the fire from now on."

"No!" Maggie answered abruptly, then she caught herself. "I mean, no, that is all right. I need to do it. It makes me feel better. I have not felt well. I feel as though my body is not my own. I feel strange all the time. I can't sleep or eat."

Frenchgirl nodded. "Have you missed your time of the moon this month?"

Maggie nodded, "Yes, for two months now. I don't feel myself. All I can think about is death."

Frenchgirl smiled. "No, Redwing, now is the time to think about life."

"What do you mean?"

Frenchgirl smiled. "Don't mothers among your people tell their daughters anything?"

"What do you mean?"

"The signs are clear, Redwing, you are carrying Firefly's baby!"

Maggie was stunned. This was the first the thought had occurred to her.

Frenchgirl was already counting on her fingers. "Your

baby will be born during the strawberry festival in early summer. This is the festival we call the celebration of the first fruits! A new life will come among us!"

Maggie stumbled off to bed, her head spinning. It was all so much.

Chapter 11

Just as Frenchgirl predicted, Maggie had her child in June, in the time of first fruits.

The birthing struck Maggie while she was in the cornfields. Frenchgirl and three other women tended to her in her time of need. At about sundown, they delivered up a Seneca, French, Irish-American baby boy.

From the first, Maggie felt her mother-love flaring up. The baby became her world. It was good to feel a new life come among them after so much death and hardship.

Maggie still made the nightly trips to Firefly's burial scaffold. It was a great comfort, during the warm summer nights, to sit under that tree and rock the baby still.

Maggie didn't think much about escaping now. She knew her boy needed the comfort and care the clan women gave. She knew she needed it too.

One evening Maggie was sitting against a tree, holding her child, when a Great Horned Owl swooped down and landed in the pine branches overhead, giving its eerie, hooting call.

The baby responded: "Hoot-hoot." For a few moments it seemed that the owl and child were in constant conversation, hooting back and forth. Then the owl flew off. The baby made its sound: "Hoot-hoot."

This was how the child got its name. Maggie called him her little Hoot Owl. Hoot Owl soon learned that he could draw a smile from any adult, even the older males, by pursing his fat, beak-like lips and saying, "Hoot-hoot."

So, Maggie thought very little about escaping. She didn't think much about the war either. She knew the Seneca and the British were fighting the Americans. But that was happening far away, somewhere to the south, and it seemed impossible that the war could reach this jewel of a valley, here in the heart of the Seneca Country. Maggie knew very little about the war and didn't care to know more. She preferred the world of growing corn and laughing babies.

The war came to Maggie's village in early September. General John Sullivan, commanding a huge army of colonists, had pushed his way north, burning the towns of the great Iroquois Confederacy. The Iroquois were simply

not equipped to stand against such a great military force.

Cornstalk came in with several other runners, early one morning, bringing the news that Sullivan's army was coming in their direction, fast.

Women and children snatched up a few essentials and made their way across the river to hide in the forest. If Sullivan destroyed their village, they knew they could head north to the British at Niagara. The men rallied to make a half-hearted stand against the huge army but decided against it.

Maggie was in the cabin when Frenchgirl came and brought the news. The women bundled up their babies and began to make for the woods. But Maggie was detained by a British officer on horse-back.

"I saw your red hair from a distance," he declared. "Where were you taken captive?"

Maggie had to think for a moment. It had been a long time since she had considered herself a captive.

"Central Pennsylvania," she said.

The officer nodded, "Good. Then you will come with me now. I will see that you get back home. We are exchanging prisoners with the Americans."

Maggie shook her head. "No, you don't understand. I don't want to go back there. I'll go to Niagara with the rest." She glanced around but she had lost sight of Frenchgirl.

The British officer dropped his courteous tone.

"This is not a request, it is a requirement. Now, you will come with me."

Maggie clutched her baby close and ran. It was easy to lose herself in the confusion. The officer was on horseback and that made it more difficult for him to maneuver.

She slipped out between the cabins and headed across the cornfields, looking for a place to hide. Then she thought of the thicket, down by the dump. She thought she could get away and hide down there.

Unfortunately, the officer saw her making her way through the dried cornstalks. He spurred his horse and chased her.

Maggie made it to the thicket and began to snake back along the trail. She stumbled into the clearing by the Rag-Picker's hut. The old woman was knelt down by the fire, surrounded by her dolls.

"Old woman," Maggie gasped, catching her breath, "I don't know if you can understand me. But if you have some power, use it against this man." She pointed to the officer, who was on foot, coming through the thicket behind her.

For a moment, Maggie stared into the Rag-Picker's eyes. There was a strange, cold gleam there, like star-light on ice.

The officer burst into the clearing, drawing his sword. He was breathing hard now.

"You will come with me," he ordered. "There is no point in running."

Maggie saw that he was right. There was no way she could get away, carrying the baby through the thicket.

"You are right," Maggie declared. "Give me a moment to change my child's clothes and I will come with you."

"No," the man said, "you will come with me alone. I have no use for the child."

Maggie stared at him in disbelief. "But I can't abandon my son."

"Very well," he said. "I will give you a choice." He strode across the clearing and snatched up one of the cornhusk dolls. "I am not a savage. I will permit you to leave your baby with this old woman."

Maggie stood firm. "No, I won't do it. You'll kill me first."

The officer chuckled. "Your life is not at stake. You are too valuable to me. Your child, on the other hand, is of no more use to me than this stupid doll."

To demonstrate his point, he held the doll out at arm's length and raised his sword, ready to sever its head.

Then, out of the corner of her eye, Maggie detected a small movement. The Rag-Picker had snatched up her walking staff and was pointing it at the officer.

Mysteriously, he dropped the doll, and lowered his sword.

In the same moment, the Rag-Picker reached over and took Hoot Owl out of Maggie's arms. Leaning on the walking stick, the old woman hugged the child to her

ragged bosom and hobbled off into the thicket.

Maggie looked after them, but they had vanished, like smoke in the wind. Then Maggie felt the officer's hands closing around her wrists, wrapping a thick chain around her hands. He grabbed the chain and dragged her out of the clearing.

The officer vaulted her up onto the horse ahead of him,

climbed on behind and they cantered up to the village, his arm encircling her body.

"You have a slim waist," the officer shouted into her ear, "I like a woman with fire in her eyes. Perhaps I'll keep you for myself."

He pulled the horse up and jumped down, pulling her with him. "But first, a little sampling of the goods. A kiss, now, and it had better be a satisfactory one."

Maggie's mind was working clearly. She lifted her chained wrists. "I would be happy to oblige you, sir, but I don't find these chains very romantic."

The officer chuckled. "On the contrary, my dear, I find them exceedingly romantic." He took a step toward her.

Maggie swung the length of chain, hard, and hit him on the side of the head, dropping him in his tracks. She turned and ran for the thicket.

She had no wish to lead anyone back to the Rag-Picker's hut. So she dashed in another direction, hiding in the thick cover down by the river until nighttime.

The next day, Sullivan's Army came. Maggie watched from the thicket as they marched, with a band playing and banners flying, into the deserted village. She had a sudden urge to walk out of the clearing and ask the soldiers for help. After all, they were her people, weren't they?

But as she watched them destroy the town, she felt

afraid of them. It took two days for the soldiers to reduce the jewel-like valley to a wasteland of smoking rubble. They chopped down the fruit trees, tore up the gardens, they threw the corn in the river or stacked it in the houses and set the buildings afire.

When the army moved on, Maggie was alone in the smokey ruin of what was once the most beautiful place she had ever seen.

But the Rag-Picker's hut was not touched. The soldiers had not gone down into the thicket. The fire, mysteriously, had not burned in that direction.

Maggie stayed at the hut for a few days, hoping the old woman would return with her son. But she didn't.

It seemed that every human being who had lived here was gone now, to another place. Just like the old woman, Maggie lived on what she could scavenge from the garbage piles at the dump. But soon, even that was not a source for food. She walked the fields but there wasn't an ear of corn or a single bean pod left to eat.

Maggie was picking through the garbage pile one night at sundown, hoping to find something to carry back to her fire, when an owl fluttered by, circling over her head. Maggie rose up out of the garbage and watched the owl. It gave an eerie cry then turned and flew south, toward the Allegheny.

Maggie hung her head. She understood. She had to go south now, toward Franny. If she stayed here through the winter, she would starve. If she went to Niagara, the British might kill or enslave her. She knew the owl was right. She would go in the morning.

Maggie felt a chill as she picked her way across the burned field to Firefly's burial scaffold. At least this

vestige of the old life was still there.

Maggie knelt and struck up the last fire she would make for her husband. She knew he would have to make cold camps the rest of the way to the Hereafter.

It started to snow a little, a November snow.

Maggie thought how strange it was: How all those months she had dreamed about escaping and heading south. And now that she was doing it, it didn't seem like she was escaping at all, she was simply wandering away.

Chapter 12

Maggie had left the village to keep from starving, but there was nothing to eat on the trail south either. She had managed to forage a few things from the Rag-Picker's hut: a little cornmeal and a small iron pot to cook it in, a moth-eaten bearskin robe to sleep in.

The snow grew deep in the woods now and it was hard walking. Maggie had wrapped her legs with blanket strips to keep warm. She wore three layers of moccasins but her feet were still wet. She spent about two hours each night drying her clothes by the fire.

Remembering the wolves, she was careful to keep the fire going and slept, off and on, wrapped up in the scrappy piece of bearskin. She wished she had an axe. The only weapon she carried was her sheath knife.

Maggie followed the waterways south, and west, retracing the route they had taken on the elk hunt. It took her six days to reach the Allegheny. The cornmeal was gone and she had taken to living on a strong tea she made by brewing pine needles in her iron pot.

Six days, walking through the deep snow on nothing but pine needle tea, Maggie came to the old Indian village site of Bucaloons, on the Allegheny River.

It had been burned to the ground and most of the rubble was covered with snow now. Maggie sifted around through the wreckage, looking for food. She had become a food-seeking animal now.

Coming down along a half-frozen stream that ran through the village, Maggie saw a conical-shaped object made from sticks lying half-submerged in the water: A fish trap!

Thinking there might be something in it, Maggie stripped off her moccasins and leg wraps and made herself wade into the frigid water, breaking the thin ice with her bare feet as she walked. There was a fish in the trap, a big one, but it had been there for a long time and had begun to rot. Maggie decided to eat it anyway.

As she was pulling the trap up out of the water, she saw something else: a familiar shape. Walking back among the ice-covered reeds she found something she had needed very badly. It was a canoe. Not one of the big, hulking

Iroquois canoes but a small, sleek Northern-style canoe, covered with birchbark.

The canoe was filled with snow. Ignoring the cold, Maggie used her hands to shovel out the loose snow, praying that the delicate craft had not been harmed. She broke the ice around the outside of the canoe with her fists and waded the canoe out of the reeds. It floated light and graceful on the icy water. Maggie smiled. She would walk in the snow no more. From here on out, the river would carry her home.

Maggie sloshed on up to the bank and built a roaring fire. The warmth came back into her feet and legs as the fish cooked over the coals. Maggie devoured it greedily and thought it was one of the best things she had ever eaten.

That night, rolled up in the bearskin in the rubble of the deserted village, Maggie slept well. She had found the fish and the canoe. It had been a good day.

In the morning, Maggie lingered by the fire, using her knife to shape up two canoe paddles from cast-off wood. She went over the canoe carefully, patching weak places in the seams with melted pine pitch. By noon she was loaded and ready to go.

She pushed off downstream and made her way down the frozen river. The force of the water was a little frightening. Maggie had to experiment with the paddle to discover a way of keeping the bow aimed into the rapids the way she had seen the Indians do. She knew that if the swirls and waves hit her broadside, they would roll the small craft over. Maggie knew that if she fell into the water, she would probably die before she could make it to shore and get a fire going. So she traveled conservatively, choosing the smoothest route down the wide, powerful waterway.

It was the day after she found the canoe that Maggie started talking to herself. When she returned to her diet of pine needle tea, something in Maggie's mind changed. She felt light-headed and giddy. She knew exactly what was happening.

"Now, Maggie," she said to herself as she paddled, "I have to have a talk with ya, dear. We can't lose touch with things now, can we? It'll only be a while more, a few more bends down the river and we'll fetch up on Kittanning, and Franny will be there. What will she think if we come up there like a blatherin' idiot? Keep a hold on yerself now!"

To calm herself, Maggie said aloud, "I'm of sound mind and body," even though she knew neither were true. "I'm of sound mind and body," she repeated. She began to sing those words as she paddled, singing them to the tune of an old hymn she remembered from her childhood. She sang to herself for hours as she paddled, sung the tune every way it could be sung, until she had the words strung out long and crazy. She sang: "I'm of sound mind and bod-ee. I'm of sound mind and bod-eee, I'm of sound mind and bod-eeeeeee!" She listened to herself and cackled wildly.

"Lord," she whispered at last, "I'm losin' my mind."

That night, like every other night, there was nothing to eat. Maggie rolled up in her bearskin by the fire. When she awoke toward midnight to build up the blaze, she was surprised to find Franny standing over her.

Maggie sat up and threw the bearskin aside.

"Franny," she asked, "how did you find me?"

But Franny didn't answer. She simply reached down to help Maggie up. Maggie reached up to grip Franny's arm but her hand went right through her, like smoke!

Maggie stood up and looked around. There was no one there.

"Maggie," she said to herself, "this is too much dear, yer seein' things now. Yer seein' things that aren't rightly here."

She laid down in the bearskin and fell back into a troubled sleep.

Maggie sang and paddled her way south all the next day. Toward twilight, she saw Franny again. This time her

aunt was standing on the shore, waving her in.

Maggie dug the paddle hard and angled the canoe over to the bank, almost upsetting in the rough water. She slipped up across the ice and into the woods, but there was no one there.

After that, Maggie made some rules for herself. She had noticed two things about the apparitions. One was that they never spoke to her. When she called to them they never answered. The other was that there was always something strange about Franny. She wasn't dressed for the weather, all she wore was an ankle-length nightdress, making her look a little like an eerie angel, appearing in the woods.

Maggie felt the mirage of her aunt standing by the fire that night but she didn't open her eyes, she didn't want to see it.

The next afternoon, she saw the apparition again. This time Franny was standing on a rock in her barefeet, waving Maggie ashore. Maggie paddled right by without stopping.

It was at about sundown on that day when Maggie thought she saw a plume of woodsmoke hanging in the sky down around the riverbend. When she rounded the bend, she could make out the shape of a log cabin, set back in the woods. But she was not convinced it was real. She pulled the canoe ashore to investigate.

As soon as she stepped up on the bank, a dog, tied to a sapling by the cabin door, started barking. Maggie had scarcely stepped from the canoe when the cabin door slid open and a rifle barrel poked out.

"What is it ya want?" a man's voice shouted.

Maggie grinned. "I'm of sound mind and body," she

said. Then she realized that had nothing to do with his question.

"What do ya want?" the voice repeated.

Maggie pulled herself together. "This must be a real place," she thought, "he's speaking."

Maggie cleared her throat. "Please sir, what is this place?"

"Kittanning. What is it ya want from us?"

"I'm starving. Can you give me something to eat?"

"What!" the man shouted, "does this look like a tavern?"

"A tavern," Maggie repeated, "yes, that's what I'm after. Is there a tavern around here?"

"About a half mile downstream, ya'll see it along the riverbank."

Maggie yipped with joy. "Is there a woman there named Franny?"

But the man had already shut the door. The dog was straining at its tether-rope now, trying to get at Maggie. She wagged her finger at the dog then turned and stepped into the canoe, pushed off downstream.

It was almost dark now. Maggie had to paddle carefully, steering clear of the rocks that jutted up through the river's surface.

Snow was falling lightly on the water now. Up ahead,

she could see the lights from the tavern windows on the water. They shone like gold coin.

"That is a real tavern," Maggie said through frozen lips, "that's a real place because that man back there was a real man and he told me it would be here."

The wind tugged at Maggie as she pulled the canoe up on shore and trudged through the deep snow up to the tavern door.

She pushed against the big oaken door but it wouldn't open, it felt as though it were bolted from inside. Maggie pounded on the door but felt as though her fists made no sound. She was so weak that she felt she might die here on the doorstep before anyone heard her. She tried to shout but her voice was thin and reedy in the wind.

Then the door opened and Maggie collapsed on the floor. She looked up and there, in the poor light, were two ghostly figures in long white robes. It was Franny and Uncle Thomas.

"Please," Maggie breathed, "please be real this time."

Then one of the visions spoke. "Come in stranger, you look froze." Maggie crawled a step ahead and Franny closed the big door behind her. By now Uncle Thomas was holding an oil lamp overhead. He pointed at her. "Look, mum . . . it's her!"

Franny bent down, "Maggie, child! You come back to us!"

Then Maggie felt the embrace: real arms and real shoulders, real hands smoothing back her hair, and real lips kissing her forehead and muttering, "Thank God, Thanks be to God in heaven fer bringin' ya to us!"

Thomas built up the fire and they drew Maggie over to the blaze, and she saw they were not wearing ghostly

robes, but white nightshirts.

"Yer real," Maggie repeated, "yer real."

Maggie fell into the warmth of her aunt's embrace and they wept.

"We been prayin' and thinkin' of ya everyday child," Franny said at last. "Wonderin' if ya were still amongst the Indians . . ."

Maggie looked up. "How did you know I was with the Indians?"

"Jake told us, dear."

"Jake. Is he here?"

"Well, surely. He's snorin' away up in the loft. He wandered in here about nine month ago, told us the whole story."

"Franny," Maggie said, "I've got a story to tell."

"Aye child, aye. And ye'll tell it, too. But first it's out of these wet clothes and into a warm nightshirt. Then it's a mug of hot cider and some Callahan Bread inta ya."

Maggie stepped out of her wet, frozen clothes and into a warm nightshirt and thick woolen socks. She devoured the food and drink Franny set before her.

But bread and cider are rich foods to a stomach that has learned to live on pine needle tea. Maggie felt a wave of nausea wash over her.

She stumbled to the tavern door. Outside, she was able to lean against a big pine tree as her stomach heaved a dozen times out into the snow. At last, Maggie felt empty and quiet inside.

Then she heard a sound in the pine branches overhead. It was the fluttering of an owl's wings.

Maggie smiled to herself. She knew that somewhere, up north, huddled in the Rag-Picker's arms, her boy was still alive. She also knew, without knowing just when, that someday she would find her little Hoot Owl and hold him in her arms again.

The End

About The Author

Robin Moore's family has lived in the mountains of Central Pennsylvania for more than 200 years, for seven generations. His ancestors were among the original settlers of the area.

Robin grew up in Boalsburg, a few miles from where Maggie's story begins, in the Seven Mountains Region of Central Pennsylvania.

As a boy, he developed an early interest in the woods and in storytelling, which he heard from his older relatives.

As an adult, he lived for two and a half years in a backwoods cabin in the Pennsylvania mountains, honing his woods skills and building a strong connection with the natural world.

Before turning to storytelling, Robin served as a

combat soldier in Vietnam, earned a journalism degree from Pennsylvania State University and worked as a newspaper reporter and magazine editor.

Robin began telling stories as a full-time profession in 1981. Since then he has presented more than 1,000 of his highly-acclaimed programs on Early American Lore at schools, museums, festivals, on radio and television. He is a frequent workshop leader on storytelling skills for parents, teachers and just plain folks.

He is owner of Groundhog Press, a small independent publishing house which produces books and tapes celebrating the oral tradition.

Robin lives with his wife, Jacqueline, and his children, Jesse and Rachel, in a stone farmhouse on a small patch of land in Montgomery County, north of Philadelphia.

About The Illustrator

William Sauts Bock has illustrated over 70 books during the past quarter century and has been honored by the *American Institute of Graphic Arts (A.I.G.A.)*, New York. He is a member of the *Philadelphia Children's Reading Round Table*, and an educator of Art, Books, and his Native American (Lenape Indian) culture.

His books include such seemingly diverse subjects as: *Crusader King, Richard the Lionhearted; Sam Adams; Tom Sawyer; The Jersey Devil; Pirates;* and *Lincoln;* as well as full color sound/film productions about Lenape culture, *Robinson Crusoe*, American Literature, ancient Greek culture, and much more.

A graduate of the Philadelphia College of Art, he is also a Lutheran minister and served as a missionary to the Navaho Indians in Arizona. He is a lecturer in American

Indian ethno-history and has traveled up and down the Susquehanna River by canoe to seek out important Indian sites. He is the friend of many American Indians and has been adopted into the Cherokee-Lenapes of Oklahoma who have given him the name of Netamuxwe.

Bock lives with his family in Souderton, Pennsylvania.

If you enjoyed this book . . .

You might be interested to know that Robin will probably continue Maggie's adventures in a third book. When this will be available, no one knows. He is a highly undisciplined and cantankerous individual and probably won't do it until he is good and ready.

If you would like to be placed on a mailing list to receive word when the third book is available, drop a line to Groundhog Press. In the meantime, you may be interested in some of the companion pieces to this book or in the first book in this series, *The Bread Sister of Sinking Creek*. An order form is enclosed at the back of the book.

ORDER FORM

Quantity	Item	Price	Total
_____	The Bread Sister	**$10.00**	_____
_____	Coloring Book	**3.00**	_____
_____	A Teaching Guide	**3.00**	_____
_____	The Bread Sister Tape	**10.00**	_____
_____	Maggie Among The Seneca	**10.00**	_____
_____	Teaching Guide	**3.00**	_____

Shipping: Add $2 on first item, 25¢ for each additional item. (Exception: Coloring Book or Guide is 50¢ on first, 25¢ on additional)   _____

Sales Tax: PA residents add 60¢ for each hardbound book or tape, 18¢ for each Guide or Coloring Book   _____

Enclosed   _____

I understand that I may return any item for a full refund if not satisfied.

Make checks payable to: Groundhog Press
Box 181, Springhouse, PA 19477

Name _____

Address _____

City _____ State _____ Zip _____